A Rancid Little Christmas

by Terry Collins
illustrated by Mel Grant

Simon Spotlight / Nickelodeon

New York   London   Toronto   Sydney   Singapore

Based on the TV series *CatDog*®
created by Peter Hannan as seen on Nickelodeon®

SIMON SPOTLIGHT
An imprint of Simon & Schuster Children's Publishing Division
1230 Avenue of the Americas, New York, New York 10020

Manufactured in the United States of America

First Edition
2 4 6 8 10 9 7 5 3 1

ISBN 0-689-83381-4

Library of Congress Catalog Card Number 00-131524

Chapter One

Christmas Eve had arrived in Nearburg, bringing along the first snowfall of the season. Snowflakes had drifted to the ground for most of the day. Now the snow had stopped falling and the entire town was draped in white.

All was quiet—except for what sounded like a pack of dogs in the distance.

They were barking and woofing in perfect harmony: "Bark, bark, bark! Woof, woof, woof! Bark, bark! Woof, woof! Bark!"

The sounds were coming from a strange-looking house high atop a cliff overlooking Nearburg. On one side the house was built in the shape of a giant fish, and on the other, a colossal bone!

On the front door was a Christmas wreath. Half the wreath had a carefully arranged fish-head pattern. The other half was covered with lopsided steak bones sloppily glued in place.

There was no doubt this was the home of Nearburg's most unusual resident, the double-headed brothers known as CatDog.

The barking stopped for a moment, then started again. Inside the house, Cat glared at Dog.

"*Enough* with the Jingle Bell Barking Choir already!" Cat pleaded as he slammed down the lid of Dog's battered record player. "You know Canine Christmas Carols always give me a headache!"

"Not if you sing them, Cat," Dog replied. "Let's warm up! La-la-la—"

"Spare me! Please . . . ," Cat begged.

"Sorry, Cat," Dog said. "I forgot you

can't bark along—you're a kitty cat!" Then he added, "We need to find you some feline Christmas carols!"

"Maybe next year. Now look, Dog. If you want to make yourself useful, plug in that string of Christmas lights." Cat pointed to a tangled mess of green wiring and colored bulbs on the floor. "At the rate we're going, we won't have this place decorated until Easter!"

When he heard the word Easter, Dog froze. "Ch-ch-ch-chocolate bunnies!" he drooled. "Yum!"

Cat shoved the lights into Dog's arms. "One holiday at a time, Dog, one holiday at a time. Untangle these and replace any burned-out bulbs. I'll start unpacking the ornaments."

Cat opened a large, faded cardboard box marked XMAS STUFF. Dog unplugged the record player and inserted the plug for the string of lights.

Instantly he was holding a festive ball of glowing red, blue, and green bulbs. "Ooooh," Dog gasped. "Pretty!"

Dog reached down and unplugged the lights. The tangled mess went dark. Dog put the plug back in. The lights sprang back to life!

Unplug. Plug. Unplug.

"Lights on, lights off," Dog whispered to himself, fascinated by his discovery. "Lights on, lights off."

Plug. Unplug. Plug. Again and again. And again.

"What's with the flashing lights!" Cat bellowed. "This ain't no disco!"

"Look, Cat! You can make them blink on and off!" Dog said, pleased with his discovery.

Cat snatched the plug out of Dog's hands. "No," he corrected wearily. "You can

electrocute yourself, that's what you can do. Now watch me. All you want to do is plug them in once, like so—"

Cat inserted the plug into the wall socket. There was a loud *crackle*, followed by a series of *pops* as each bulb on the strand shorted out!

"Yeow!" Cat shrieked. His fur stood on end, charged with sizzling electricity.

Then finally jerking the plug out of the wall, Cat exclaimed, "Whew! That was close! I think I singed my whiskers! You okay, Dog?"

Dog looked at Cat with a vacant grin. "Scalp feels all . . . tingly," he said.

Cat hurled the ball of now-blackened bulbs into a corner. "So much for lights on the tree this year," he said sadly. "We're too poor to buy new ones."

"Aw, cheer up, Cat," Dog replied.

"We've still got lots of great ornaments."

Dog stuck his head into the cardboard box and fetched a delicate glass ornament in the shape of a purple flounder. "Thee? Thook! Thoor thavorite!" he said.

"What? I can't understand a word you're—," Cat muttered, turning around to see what Dog was holding. "Oh, no!"

Dog opened his mouth. "I said, See? Look! Your—"

The glass flounder plummeted from Dog's mouth. *Crash!*

"Favorite," Dog finished softly. "Sorry, Cat."

Chapter Two

Dog waited for Cat to start yelling at him. Instead, Cat calmly led Dog into the kitchen, picked up a broom and dustpan, and stepped back into the living room.

"Hold this," Cat said, giving Dog the dustpan. "We need to sweep up *all* the glass."

"Gee, Cat . . . I didn't mean to—," Dog began, but Cat cut him off with a look.

"This was an accident, Dog," Cat said reassuringly, brushing the broken purple fragments into a neat and tidy pile. "You didn't drop the precious antique flounder I've owned since I was a kitten on purpose. I know that."

"Well, yeah . . . ," Dog said. "Um . . . cheer up, Cat!"

"Why?"

Dog paused. "You just got to—it's Christmas Eve!"

Cat shrugged. "So? Another broke holiday. Whoopee."

Dog lowered his eyes. "I said I was sorry about your fishie, Cat."

Cat put his arm around Dog's shoulders. "Not the flounder, Dog. That's not the kind of broke I meant."

"Oh, okay," Dog replied, then looked puzzled.

"I was speaking of being broke as in a lack of funds," Cat explained. Dog still looked confused. Cat tried again. "We have an absence of *moolah*."

Dog nodded, but still didn't understand. Cat sighed. "We have NO MONEY, Dog!"

"Ohhhh!" Dog exclaimed, finally

comprehending. "Well, gosh, Cat . . . we *never* have any money!"

"Exactly!" Cat cried. "Every year at Christmas, it's the same old story! No cash to travel! Crummy homemade presents under the Christmas tree! No credit cards to use for after-Christmas sales! Zip. Zilch! ZERO!"

Dog scratched one of his ears and said in a quiet voice, "But, Cat, Christmas *isn't* about money."

Cat slapped a hand to his own forehead. "Well, duh, Dog, I know that! But being broke is still a lousy way to celebrate the holiday season!"

"That's a real news flash!" a voice said. "I live under the same roof as you guys, and you still won't scrape together enough coins to send me a Christmas card."

It was Winslow, a small, rodentlike,

blue creature who made his home in the walls of CatDog's house. Dog counted Winslow as a loyal friend, but Cat hated him because Winslow was a freeloader who had a knack for appearing at the worst possible moments.

"Why should we?" Cat sneered. "You've never bought us a card."

"Sure I have!" Winslow corrected, pointing to a worn card tacked to the mantle.

"Winslow, you've been giving us this same card for years," Cat said. "You just cross out the old year and write in the new one before sticking it in Dog's stocking!"

"So? Recycling is a very good thing," Winslow replied.

As Cat and Winslow argued, Dog thought about Cat's words. Suddenly an idea popped into his tiny canine brain.

"Cat! I know how we can have lots of

Christmas fun *without* any money!"

Cat sat down on his side of the sofa (the clean and well-groomed half). "If it involves more of those barking Christmas carols, count me out."

Dog hopped up beside his brother on the other half of the sofa (the chewed and smelly side). He wiggled with delight.

Cat peered into Dog's big soft eyes. "I know that look. You have an idea, don't you?"

Dog giggled. "Uh-huh! Uh-huh!"

"I know I'm going to regret this . . . but what?" Cat asked.

"We can go sledding up on Bonebreak Bluff and still be back in plenty of time to put out Christmas punch and dog biscuits for Santy Claus!" Dog said in a torrent of words.

Cat brightened. "Say! You're right,

Dog! Half of Nearburg gathers at Bonebreak Bluff on the night of the first big snow! It might be fun!"

"I could use a change in routine myself!" Winslow added. "Count me in. I'll be back as soon as I put on my winter coat!"

CatDog dressed in their warmest scarves before walking outside to fetch their U-shaped homemade sled. After tugging it out from under the front porch, Cat was relieved to find the wooden sled still in working condition.

"Ready, Dog?" Cat asked.

Dog looked back at the house. "I wonder what's taking Winslow so long?" he asked.

"Who cares?" Cat said. "He can find his own way!"

Chapter Three

Numerous Nearburg citizens were already there and sledding when CatDog reached the top of Bonebreak Bluff. Cat stopped to catch his breath and asked Dog, "Does this sled seem heavier to you than last year?"

"Sorta, kinda . . . well, yeah," Dog replied.

They turned to find a tiny blue stowaway sitting on the sled!

"W-W-Win-Winslow!" Cat sputtered.

"Hi-ya, CatDog," Winslow replied. "Thanks for the swell taxi service!"

"Let me give you a head start on the return trip—" Cat snarled, grabbing Winslow and threatening to hurl him back down the mountain.

"Cat! No!" Dog protested, arching his

back to tip Cat off balance. Cat dropped Winslow and all three of them toppled over into the snow.

"Yeah, easy there, pussycat! You're wrinkling my winter wardrobe," Winslow cracked.

"Maybe if I squash you flat, that would take care of the problem," Cat suggested.

"Easy, Cat," said Dog. "It's Christmas. Besides, Winslow is our friend."

"*Your* friend, Dog," Cat corrected.

Winslow ignored Cat. "Hey, I'm a nice guy. I'll let my free ride be your Christmas gift to me."

"Isn't that nice of Winslow, Cat?" Dog asked, as the little blue creature walked away to get a ride with other sledders.

Cat harumphed. "Let's just get this ride over with. I'm freezing."

CatDog stood in line at the top of the

bluff and waited their turn. Just then a muscular dog in a leather jacket joined them. "Well, well, well . . . look who crawled outta their hidey-hole to enjoy the Christmas festivities," he sneered.

They spun around to face Cliff, leader of the notorious Greaser dogs. The Greasers were bullies who liked nothing better than to pound on CatDog.

And where Cliff went, his two side-kicks, Shriek and Lube, were sure to follow.

"What, no hug for your old pal?" Cliff asked, reaching out to grab CatDog.

"Run!" Cat yelled, only to find their escape route blocked by Shriek!

"Not so fast, cutie," the white poodle said, tickling Dog under the chin. "We haven't even stood under the mistletoe yet."

"Uh, yeah, time to toe the missile, or something," Lube added.

"Great," Cat sobbed, placing his face in his paws. "What would my Christmas Eve be without a visit from the Greasers?"

"My point exactly, Cat!" Shriek said, slapping his back. "Tradition is tradition."

"And, uh, we got you a Christmas present, too," Lube said.

Cat and Dog exchanged nervous looks.

"Is it the same thing you gave us last year?" Cat asked.

"Yup!" Cliff replied.

"Let's run, Dog!" cried Cat, taking off, but not before Cliff grabbed Dog by his paws.

Cat struggled to get away, but Cliff's grip on Dog was too strong. Finally Cliff let go, and CatDog hurtled backward into the snow.

Shriek and Lube started laughing hysterically.

Poking his head up from under a pile of snow, Cat glared at Dog. "I could be at home right now, having a miserable but warm and pain-free Christmas Eve," he said. "But noooo, you had to drag us up here!"

"It could have been worse, Cat," said Dog. "They could have thumped us—"

"Quiet!" Cat snapped. "Don't give them any ideas!"

"Once you stop hurting, we'll take our sled ride," Dog said.

"I'm used to pain," Cat retorted. "Let's go!"

But their sled was nowhere to be found!

Chapter Four

"Our sled!" Cat cried, as Dog dug frantically in the snow. But the sled had vanished!

"Can this Christmas get *any* worse?" Cat moaned.

"Cat! Look!" Dog said, pointing. Perched on one another's shoulders like a totem pole were the Greasers. The trio was preparing to go down the hill—on CatDog's sled!

"Hey!" Cat cried out. "That's our property!"

"Finders, keepers!" Shriek taunted from atop her perch. "But we're not selfish!"

"Yeah, you're more than welcome to *watch* us use it. Haw, haw, haw!" Cliff added.

"Uh, upsy-daisy," Lube said and pushed them off. The Greasers waved good-bye as they slid down the hill.

"Guess we get to walk home," Cat said.

"We don't need a sled, Cat!" Dog replied. "We can use our belly!"

Cat looked at his tummy. "I dunno, Dog. That snow looks pretty cold."

"You won't feel a thing," Dog said. "Let's give it a try!"

"I know I won't feel anything . . . my stomach will be numb," Cat began to say, just before Dog leaped into the air! Seconds later—*ploomph!*—they landed in a spray of white. CatDog slid quickly down the hill, their scarves flapping in the breeze.

Cat opened one eye. "Dog, I don't say this very often," he yelled, "but you were right! This is bee-yoo-tee-ful!"

Whump! CatDog crashed into a large rock! They flew into the air again, then plunged into the snow and started to roll down the hill like a runaway doughnut!

CatDog picked up snow and became a snowball that grew and grew as it rolled down the hill.

"Hi-ho-diggety!" Dog yelled. Cat tried to scream, but got a mouthful of snow instead.

The snowball was now six feet high, with an ear sticking out here, a foot sticking out there, and no brakes!

Halfway down the hill, the Greasers were slowly making their way back to the top after their ride. Lube was pulling Cliff and Shriek on CatDog's sled.

"You're doing fine work, Lube," Cliff told him.

"Yeah, and next time, we'll give *you* a lift to the top," Shriek said with a snicker.

Suddenly Lube stopped pulling. "Uh, something's coming," he said.

"Delays, delays," Shriek said. "Just hurry it up already. We have to head home or Santy Claus won't come and visit us!"

"Wait, Lube's right," Cliff said. "I can hear it too! A rumbling noise."

The sound got louder as the snowball approached.

"Avalanche!" Cliff yelled. "Run!"

The Greasers never stood a chance. The snowball, now the size of a small house, rolled over and snatched them up!

Hopping over a fence, the runaway snowball cruised down Main Street! Last-minute shoppers ran for their lives as the rolling mass of snow, ice, and animals crushed the roofs of parked cars and ripped down power lines.

At the end of Main Street was a skyscraper—and the immense snowball was headed right for it!

When it hit the front doors, the snow-ball broke apart, scattering mounds of ice and snow—along with CatDog and the Greasers—in all directions through the building's lobby.

As CatDog, Lube, Cliff, and Shriek popped up dazedly out of the snow, they shouted at each other.

"This is all *your* fault!"

"*You* were driving the snowball!"

"You stole *our* sled!"

"No way! We *borrowed* it!"

Just then the arguing was interrupted by a loud *ding*. Elevator doors opened to reveal a peeved Rancid R. Rabbit.

"What's with the racket?" he demanded. "How can a wealthy businessman like myself count his Christmas profits in peace?"

Chapter Five

"Look at my beautiful lobby! My carpet! My paintings! My corporate awards! Ruined!" Rancid Rabbit ranted. "*Someone* is going to pay for this mess!"

"Why did I give security the night off for Christmas?" he continued, whipping out a small tape recorder. "Memo," Rancid said into the recorder. "Never, *ever*, allow security to leave the premises again!"

"Look, Dog!" Cat whispered, gesturing at a mound of snow by the elevator. Sticking out of the pile was their sled!

"Sled, sled, sled," Dog chanted softly.

"I'll distract the rabbit, you snag our *prop-per-tay*," Cat said.

"Okeydokey!" Dog agreed.

Cat assumed his best fighting posture and faced Rancid. "Look, mister. What you've got here is an act of, um, natural events. Nobody's fault. Avalanches happen."

"We'll see what my attorney says about that," Rancid retorted. "I've got all this on video!"

While Rancid yelled, Dog twisted around and got his hands on the sled. As he pulled it free, someone else stepped out into the lobby.

Dog's mouth fell open. He reached over and started tugging at the cuff of Rancid's tailored trousers.

"I'll sue all of you! I'll—what do you want? Get your hands off me!" Rancid shouted.

Dog looked up at Rancid with a sly expression. "You'd better be nice, or—"

"Or what?" Rancid sneered.

"Well, you-know-who is right behind

you, and he knows if you're being naughty or nice," Dog answered in a singsong voice.

Cat, the Greasers, and Rancid all turned. Standing in the shadows near the elevator was . . . Santa Claus!

Chaos erupted as the Greasers cried, "Santy Claus!" Pushing, shoving, and climbing over each other, they scrambled toward Santa, only to slip on the wet lobby floor.

The Greaser dogs crashed into the bearded gentleman, knocking him off his feet. "Oof!" Santa exclaimed.

"Didja get my letter?" Cliff asked as he got up and helped Santa into a chair.

"What, you can write now?" Shriek retorted. "I know Santy Claus got my letter because I sent it overnight mail to the North Pole!"

"Uh, I, um, sent Santa an E-mail," Lube said proudly.

"Friends, please," Santa said, holding up his gloved hands. "I received your letters, but I can't talk now. I have to hurry or Nearburg won't be celebrating Christmas at all!"

"What do you mean?" Cat asked with a nervous chuckle. "You're Santa Claus. Delivering presents all over the world in a single night is no big deal for you."

"Not this year," Santa said sadly. "I fear come Christmas Day, I might be out of a job!"

Dog laid his chin on Santa's knee. "No more Santy Claus?"

"Yeah!" Rancid sneered. "I've decided to take out the jolly, old, fat middleman! After tonight, a good old-fashioned Christmas goes the way of the plaid leisure suit! By this time next year, *I'll* be calling the shots!"

Chapter Six

"You must be joking," Cat said in disbelief to Rancid. Dog and the Greasers all bobbed their heads in agreement.

"Rabbits never joke!" Rancid replied, pointing a long green finger in Cat's face. "I have the merchandise ready to ship! And it's *my* kind of merchandise—building blocks made of used cardboard instead of wood! Boring textbooks instead of stereo equipment! And best of all . . . extra squishy stuffed animals filled with moldy old oatmeal!"

"Santy Claus, is this true?" Dog asked.

"Yes, Dog, I'm afraid it is," Santa replied.

Rancid held out a contract. "Your overstuffed hero's deal for Christmas with the Holiday Authority clearly states that if *all* deliveries are not made by sunrise, the job is up for grabs!"

Santa looked sheepish as he took in all of the sad faces in the lobby.

"But—but you can't take Christmas away from Santa Claus!" Cat exclaimed.

"Wise up!" Rancid said. "Jolly Old Saint Nick here is ready to fall through the holiday cracks."

"You're cruisin' for a bruisin', rabbit," Cliff threatened. "You *can't* mess with Christmas!"

"Sure I can," Rancid retorted. "I made a fortune on Easter last year. Remember *solid* pure milk chocolate Easter eggs? Gone. I'm the guy who switched them with *hollow* artificial chocolate! Saved a bundle!"

Rancid continued to brag. "Fake grass in Easter baskets? My idea. And this year

I'm introducing painted replica jelly beans!"

CatDog and the Greasers were stunned. Finally Cat asked, "You mean—"

"That I'm the new Easter Bunny?" Rancid said. "You betcha. One holiday down, an entire calendar to go! I'm going to be king of all holidays! Now, if you'll excuse me, I've got an image to develop—Santa Rabbit," Rancid mused as he got onto the elevator. "Hmm . . . I like the sound of it!"

Shaking his head, Santa walked outside and sat down on the curb. CatDog and the Greasers followed him.

"Oh, that Rancid," Santa sighed. "He's been like this since he was a baby bunny . . . always looking out for himself. He never did learn that Christmas is about doing good deeds, loving everyone, and celebrating the spirit of the season."

"Why worry about this clown trying

to muscle into *your* territory, Santy?" Shriek asked. "You can take care of him easy!"

"Normally, that would be true. But Nearburg was the last stop on my delivery list," Santa explained. "Rancid knew this, and when I arrived, he had my sleigh, the contents, and my eight reindeer impounded."

Santa started pacing back and forth on the sidewalk. "That rabbit made up some nonsense about not having the proper license to fly a sleigh at night! Now I can't use the sleigh in Nearburg except in the daytime!"

"You want us to go beat him up?" Cliff asked, cracking his knuckles.

"We know how to make him change his mind," Shriek agreed ominously.

"I appreciate that," Santa told them. "But violence really isn't my way of doing things. I'm stuck with no sleigh, no reindeer, and no presents! If I don't get gifts under every tree in Nearburg tonight, the consequences could be disastrous for Christmas!"

"We'll help you deliver the presents, Santy Claus!" Dog said.

"Count the Greasers in, too!" Cliff said. "No funny bunny's going to wreck our fun."

"But my friends, we'll have to *make* the presents before we can deliver them," Santa said. "And my elves are thousands of miles away at the North Pole."

"That's okay, Santa," Cat replied with a grin. "We've got a few elves of our own we can call on!"

Chapter Seven

Back at home, CatDog set up Santa's workshop in their living room.

Everyone they knew answered the plea for help. Under Santa's watchful eye, Eddie the Squirrel, Mr. Sunshine, Winslow, the Greasers—and even Randolph worked hard to make toys and gifts for delivery that night.

CatDog had everything they needed to make presents. Empty dog food cans became the wheels of toy cars, and old fish skeletons made wonderful, educational model kits!

Randolph had brought a stack of photographs of himself and gave each one a lipstick kiss before wrapping it up and adding it to the pile of presents. Mr. Sunshine used a power saw to cut up scrap lumber into small wooden building blocks. They were then passed along to Winslow to add letters and numbers to the sides.

The Greasers turned out to be skilled painters, quickly spray painting all items sent their way. "I knew all that graffiti we did would come in handy!" Shriek said to her pals.

"Hey, Cat, here's something else we can give away," Dog said, holding up a cardboard box he'd found in Cat's bedroom closet. "You've never even opened this old doll of yours!"

"Are you nuts?" Cat hissed, snatching away the toy. "No way, Dog! Not my mint-in-the-box, Mean Bob action figure! He stays with *me*."

"But, Cat, you've never even played

with him . . . and out there is a little child just dying to set Mean Bob free on Christmas morning," Dog whined.

Cat gritted his teeth . . . and finally added Mean Bob to the pile of toys to be wrapped. "I'm proud of you, Cat!" Dog said.

"So am I," Santa added.

Cat smiled, embarrassed and trying not to think of his favorite action figure.

As the pile of presents grew, Santa's heart began to fill with hope. Perhaps they would be able to make the deliveries tonight after all! He took out his list of names and checked it twice.

Santa then blew his whistle. "We've done it! We have enough presents for all of Nearburg!" he announced. Everyone cheered.

Santa blew the whistle again. "Now we have to deliver them," he said.

Everyone carried the wrapped gifts outside to Randolph's mail truck. Once the truck was loaded, there was hardly any room for passengers!

Randolph turned the key and the starter made a clicking noise.

"Sounds like a dead battery to me," Mr. Sunshine said in a monotone.

"We need a tow," Randolph said.

"On Christmas Eve? At this time? Get real!" Cat retorted.

"Then we've got to pull it into Nearburg ourselves," Dog said.

"I'll get some rope," Cat said, sighing.

After tying the rope to the bumper of the truck, everyone, even Winslow, began to pull. Santa sat behind the wheel of the truck to steer.

Luckily for everyone, once the truck started rolling, it was able to coast the rest of the way down into the city limits. Santa parked the truck and handed out assignments and gifts.

"Uh, everybody's sleepin'. How we gonna get into the houses?" Lube asked.

"Through the chimney, you dope," Shriek said. "Right, Santa?"

Santa shrugged. "It always worked for me," he said.

Everyone split up into teams. Mr. Sunshine and Winslow took the first house. But rather than climbing onto the roof and going down the chimney, Mr. Sunshine opened the front door with a key and walked in!

"Hey! You want to get us arrested?" Winslow asked in alarm.

"There's no need for rooftop acrobatics," Mr. Sunshine replied. "My uncle is a locksmith. I'm using his master key."

"Sweet!" Winslow said, beaming. "Sunny boy, this is the beginning of a beautiful friendship!"

Across the street, the Greasers were trying to lower Lube down the chimney—when the roof caved in. Luckily, they landed on something soft. Unluckily, it was the owner of the house, who also happened to be Nearburg's dogcatcher.

"Merry Christmas?" Cliff said in a small voice as the net fell over his shoulders.

Meanwhile, Randolph left his gifts in everyone's mailboxes. He merrily deposited pictures of himself until he ran out.

"Oops. Gotta go home and restock!" he said, and jogged down the sidewalk.

CatDog delivered their presents the old-fashioned way. Dog hung on to the lip of the chimney of their chosen home while lowering Cat down to the fireplace.

"A little further, Dog," Cat whispered. "I can almost see the tree!"

Dog stretched and Cat's head poked into the room. In Cat's hands was a gift for a little girl named Ginny.

And this little girl was now standing by the Christmas tree with a tray of cookies, a glass of milk, and a shocked expression.

"Ho-ho-ho?" Cat said weakly.

Chapter Eight

"What are *you* . . . some kind of wood-chuck?" Ginny asked in a loud whisper.

"Not hardly," an insulted Cat retorted. "What are you still doing up?"

Ginny gave Cat a pitying look. "I'm waiting for Santa Claus, dummy."

"Well, uh, I'm him. Santa Claus, I mean," Cat announced. "And you should be in bed, young lady!"

The little girl peered into the fireplace. "If you're Santa, what's with the orange fur coat?" she asked. "You're supposed to be wearing red."

"Mrs. Claus faded it in the wash, okay? Now scram, or I won't put your present under the tree!" Cat snapped.

But Ginny didn't scram. Instead, she came closer. On her feet were fuzzy, brown bunny slippers. "Here," she said, handing Cat the tray. "I made you a snack."

Cat was touched. "Great!" he said as he took the glass. "I loooove milk!"

Ginny tiptoed back to her bedroom, as Cat tried to figure out how to drink the milk while upside down. But before he could take a sip, Dog jerked him back up to the roof. The glass of milk spilled all over Cat's face!

"You couldn't have given me another sixty seconds?" the drenched Cat asked.

"My back was killing me!"

CatDog trudged back to the truck to get another present to deliver. Santa joined them.

"Where is everybody?" Cat asked as he licked milk from his fur.

Santa shrugged. "I think we're the only two left, boys."

"I resent that remark," a tiny voice said from under the van. Winslow looked up. "I'm here, but Mr. Sunshine's down for the count. He took a break on somebody's kitchen table and started snoring."

Santa reached into his red coat and took out a gold pocket watch. "The sun rises in less than ten minutes. Without my reindeer and sleigh, I can't move fast enough to hit every house."

"There's got to be a way we can pull this off," Cat said. The face of the little girl appeared in his mind. He didn't want to disappoint other children!

Then another face appeared with the little girl. Two brown fuzzy faces, actually.

"Hold on, Santa! I just had a turr-rrific idea!" Cat said. "Come on, Dog! We've got to find a pay phone!"

CatDog ran around the corner, and in

a near instant, reappeared with a new ally.

"Well, I'll be!" Santa said with delight. "Where did you find *him?*"

"I've got connections," Cat replied, taking a moment to bask in a job well done.

"And a phone book!" Dog added.

"We looked under Bunnies for Hire, and there he was!" Cat admitted.

"Hi, Marty," Santa said, shaking the new arrival's paw. "Still hopping, I see."

"Hello, Kris," replied the Easter Bunny. "Don't know how you can stand the cold. At least I've got a fur coat!"

"Wow, the Easter Bunny!" Winslow said, impressed. "I've been a fan since I was three years old. Love your work."

"Ex-Easter Bunny," the rabbit said sadly. "I quit in disgust!"

"I thought being an Easter Bunny was a lifetime gig," Cat said.

The Easter Bunny rubbed one of his long floppy ears. "Rancid Rabbit is my second cousin on my mother's side," he explained. "He expressed an interest in the family business, so I took him in. Before I knew what was happening, he had taken over so *everything* was done his way!"

Santa shook his head. "Rancid was always on my naughty list."

"Well, he's in for a fight come this Easter! I'm taking my old job back!" the Easter Bunny said firmly. "And I'm more than willing to help save Christmas from the likes of him."

In a flash, the Easter Bunny pitched in with his super-quick delivery abilities, dropping off the presents on Santa's list faster than the speed of light.

But . . . was it already too late?

Chapter Nine

Inside his penthouse suite, Rancid Rabbit waited with anticipation in a plush easy chair beside his Christmas tree. There were no presents under the eight-foot tree, nor were there any stockings on the mantle over the fireplace.

Rancid was anxiously staring at the clock. In less than sixty seconds, the sun would be coming up, and Santa would no longer have anything to do with Christmas.

The rabbit smiled. First Easter, now Christmas . . . and in the future, well, he'd been keeping tabs on Halloween. Witches and ghosts had always made Rancid nervous, but now he thought he could get the better of them.

"I'll use high school talent show winners," Rancid said. "Even Halloween spooks are scared of bad tap-dancing routines and off-key Broadway show tunes!"

Just then a blur whipped past. "Brrrr," Rancid said, pulling his robe around his shoulders. "Must be a draft."

He glanced down at the tree, and was shocked to see a present. Picking up the box, Rancid read the card, "To Rancid, From Santa."

"Leaping lumbago!" Rancid said as he rechecked the clock. He got up, and pulled the curtains off the window. The sky was still dark! Santa must have gotten all the presents out before the deadline!

"ARRRRGH!" Rancid screamed. "I don't believe it! How could he have beaten me?"

The rabbit flopped down in his chair

with a moan. He looked at the present.

Suddenly he got very curious. Ripping away the festive wrapping paper, he opened the box to find . . . five lumps of shiny black coal. Rancid held up one of the lumps and fought back tears of happiness.

"It—it's what he gets me every year," he said with a relieved sigh. Rancid now knew that despite all his attempts to steal Christmas, Santa didn't hold a grudge.

The rabbit happily placed each lump on the table next to the tree.

"Merry Christmas, Santa," he whispered as he watched the sun rise slowly into the sky.

Chapter Ten

Back on the other side of Nearburg, Santa and CatDog also watched as the sun rose, knowing that Christmas had arrived safely.

Santa gave a wide yawn and stretched. "That's another one down, boys," he said with a wink. "I just hope the Easter Bunny didn't leave any marshmallow eggs or chocolate bunnies by mistake!"

"Where'd he go, anyway?" Cat asked.

"Why, hopping down the bunny trail, of course," Santa grinned. "And I should be on my way as well. Mrs. Claus gets worried if I'm not home by sunup!"

Santa climbed into his sleigh. Now that day had arrived, he could use it again.

"So, this is it, I guess," Dog said.

"Never fear, Dog. Next year will be here before you know it," Santa replied. "Thank you both for helping to save Christmas."

"Pshaw, it was nothing," Cat said, trying not to blush.

"I owe you a debt of thanks," Santa replied. "But for now, you'll just have to make do with the presents I left at your house."

"*Presents?*" CatDog said in unison. "For *us?*"

"For you. And remember, boys . . . be good, for goodness sake!" Santa said with a smile. "Now stand back and give me room."

CatDog watched as Santa gave a gentle tug on the reins of his sleigh team. The eight reindeer kicked their feet and his now-empty sled rose effortlessly into the air.

CatDog waited outside a long time,

waving until they could no longer see Santa's sleigh.

Then CatDog ran into their house. "Come on, Dog! Let's check out the tree!" Cat said. The clutter and debris from the night before had vanished. Now their Christmas tree was fully decorated in half-Cat and half-Dog style, just like all of their other possessions.

Even better, the tree was complete with blinking lights! And under the tree were two gaily-wrapped packages.

"To Dog, From Santa," Dog read, picking up a large boxed present. He ripped the paper off, revealing a dinosaur-sized bone!

"Wow!" Dog exclaimed as he started to drool. "A bone!"

"So that's what you get for the dog who has everything," Cat said with a chuckle

as he carefully unwrapped his own gift, taking care not to crease the ribbon. "Don't know what mine is . . . it's too small to be a Mean Bob action figure."

Inside was an ornament made of purple antique spun glass. "My Christmas flounder! Bee-yoo-tee-ful!" Cat said in amazement. He hung the ornament on the tree.

"See! I told you Christmas isn't about money," Dog said.

"You were right. This was *much* better than cash," Cat agreed.

Standing back from the tree, CatDog took in the festive sight.

"Merry Christmas, Cat!" Dog said with a smile.

"Same to you, Dog," Cat replied. "Same to you."

About the Author

As a child, Terry Collins always suspected Santa Claus and the Easter Bunny were friends. Now that he's all grown up, he's glad to know he was right! However, he's still not sure if they hang out with the Tooth Fairy. . . .

Terry has written hundreds of stories for children—many featuring characters from Nickelodeon. This is his second book about the world of CatDog and their friends. Terry lives in North Carolina with his wife, Ginny, and their four dogs—who shed entirely too much on the furniture.